THE RUNAWAY PEA LEFT BEHIND

Kjartan Poskitt and Alex Willmore

SIMON & SCHUSTER

London   New York   Sydney   Toronto   New Delhi

We're on the way back
from a big shopping trip –
but the bag's caught a nail
and it's started to rip.

Dropetty

PLOP!

Now what could that be?

All on his own, it's a left-behind pea.

"Help!" the pea shouted.
"Don't go without me!"

But the carrots
all laughed,
"It's your fault –
don't you see?

If you weren't so tiny, you wouldn't fall through.
You're too small to matter – we can't wait for you."

The left-behind pea gave a sorrowful sigh,
and watched as the feet and the pushchairs went by.

"Who wants to go home in a bag anyway?
I'd rather be small and have fun any day!"

Suddenly, down came
a boot with a **BUMP!**

It shook up the ground
and it made the pea **JUMP!**

Then right out of nowhere
a skateboard came past.
The pea landed on it
and shot off so FAST . . .

WHIZZITY-WHIZZLE and ZIGGETY-ZAG!

It was far better fun
being out of the bag!

CLACKETY-CLACK

down some steps the board skipped.

But when it got

down to the bottom

it FLIPPED...

The little pea pinged up surprisingly high,
just as the number ten bus tootled by.

The pea hit the screen
with a bit of a **SPLAT,**
but though he was shaken
he didn't mind that . . .

. . . 'cos **BRUMM** went the engine.
"Hooray!" said the pea.

"I'm getting a
ride, everyone –
look at ME!"

Riding the bus
he felt ever so proud,
but as he toured round
the pea saw a dark cloud.

It started to rain and the wipers came on –
then one mighty swish, and the pea ... he was gone!

The pea hit a tree, he bounced this way and that,
then fell in a nest where a nightingale sat.

The curious bird stood and lifted her leg
and found she had one extra little green egg.
"Hello!" said the pea, with a big cheeky grin.
"I saw you were home so I thought I'd drop in."

But the pea had got tangled in feathery fluff,

and up blew a breeze with a

HUFF and a PUFF!

The nightingale stepped back and waved a goodbye,

as the pea drifted upwards off into the sky.

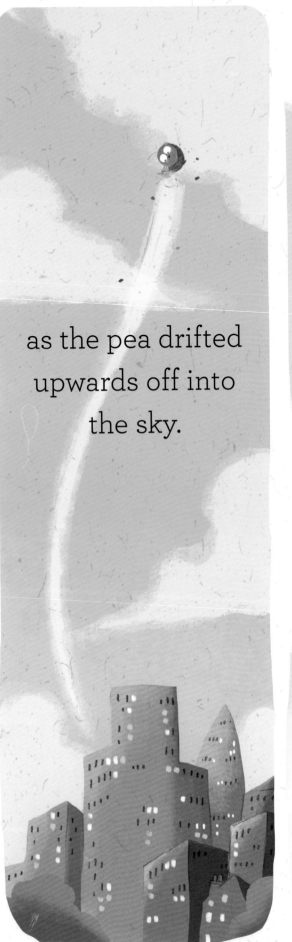

Higher and higher he started to soar – higher than any pea had been before.

He cried out with joy looking down at the view
of houses and rooftops and chimney pots, too.

"Oh, what a wonderful day for a pea,
when everything everywhere's smaller than me!"

Below was a pitch with a game underway.
"What fun!" said the pea. "I so wish I could play."

He wriggled around to keep watching the ball,
but the fluff came untangled and . . .

... let the pea fall!

"ARGHHH!" cried the pea as he felt himself dropping, with no way of steering and no way of stopping.

He closed his eyes tight and just hoped for the best as he crashed through the tree, past the nightingale's nest.

Suddenly ...

...SPLOTT! But where was he now?

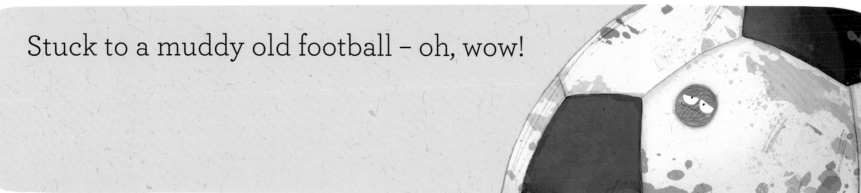
Stuck to a muddy old football – oh, wow!

PEEP went a whistle,
then BIFF went a boot.
And straight at the goal mouth
the football did shoot!

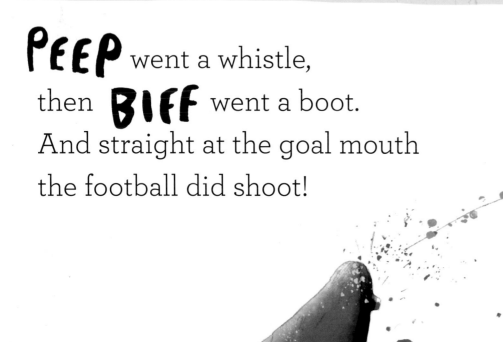

The crowd who were watching
all gave a great roar.
"HOORAY!" the pea shouted.
"I'm going to score."

But the net had a hole
and the ball didn't stop
'til it hit a sharp spike
on the fence and went

The pea was sent flying so hard by the blast that he knocked off a flowerpot – **SMASH** – as he passed.

He flew in a door and went **BING** off a light,

and then **BANG** on a pan, giving Boris a fright.

He bounced off a washing bag full of old socks
and rolled to a stop in a big wooden box.

His fun was all finished. He felt so dejected . . .

. . . then got a strange feeling
that he'd been expected.

"Hello!" said a bean.
"How d'ya do?" said a sprout.
"This is where ALL the
cool veggies hang out."

But then overhead, they all heard a loud rumbling,
and out of the shopping bag, carrots came tumbling.

"GET OUT OF OUR WAY!"

they yelled out
as they fell.

"We're fresh from the shops but the rest of you smell."
"That's rude!" said the sprout. "And it's not even true.
We've got a new friend here who's fresher than you!"

The carrots complained, "It's the pea! That's unfair. We left you behind us. How did you get there?"

As everyone waited, the pea glowed with pride. "I just found a quicker way home," he replied.

"I skated, then rode on a bus,

then I flew,

then I scored a quick goal and got here before you."

"Nonsense!" the carrots all cackled with scorn.
But the pea shook his head and he did a big yawn.

"Don't be so jealous of one little pea.
I'm too small to matter, is what you told me.

But small as I am, I do like to have fun –
and it's been a long day so goodnight, everyone!"